Prairie Storms

by Darcy Pattison
illustrated by Kathleen Rietz

Low, thick clouds dump snow, covering the prairies. Whistling winds shape and mold the snow into drifts and hollows. The prairie chicken claws into a drift, digging a winter roost.

January

The hibernating ground hog stirs, awakes. It unplugs the door to its den and peers out. Soft billows of fog blot out the sun.

February

Migrating sandhill cranes sail down, seeking safety from strange winds that twist and twirl. Nervous, they wade and call. Overhead, a tornado roars past, sweeping across the open lands.

March

Rain and rain and rain and—it's a flash flood! Walls of water crash through the prairie dog town. Deep in the muddy burrows, prairie dog families hunker, safe in pockets of air— until the waters go down.

April

May

After an evening shower, a red fox trots through the still-wet meadows. It stalks a mouse and eats. Then it blankets itself with its bushy tail and sleeps amidst the soft, spring flowers.

Puffy morning clouds build and build all afternoon until thunderclouds tower high. Flash! Boom! The white tailed doe and fawn both flee, helter-skelter, toward a tree.

June

July

After weeks of no rain and a baking sun, the land is parched. Dry summer winds gather up dirt and whip into a dust storm. The striped skunk bars its doorway with rough balls of straw. Even then, dust creeps into the den, turning black and white fur to brown.

August

Still no rain. Clouds gather, but in this heat wave, the air just crackles with dry lightning. Flash! Flash! Flash! In the dry sandy soil, the earless lizard shimmies and disappears beneath the surface.

September

The burrowing owl chicks have grown and flown. But the mama and papa owl still linger near their underground nest. A sudden cloudburst drums the land, spreading an early autumn chill. And when a rainbow arches the sky, it's time. The burrowing owls take wing and fly toward warmer lands.

October

One night, thunder echoes and autumn winds wail. Suddenly, hail stones pound the ground. Caught in the open, the cougar dashes to his den. Hidden beneath a wide ledge, he watches and gnaws on dry and brittle bones.

Icy needles of sleet coat the dried grasses and weigh down the trees. The bald eagle clenches its branch, enduring, letting its wings shed the sleet. When the storm passes, the eagle preens, then soars to hunt.

November

A blizzard rages, a sudden whiteout. The bison herd turns, facing into the teeth of the wind. The herd stands, unshaken, unmovable, undaunted. The bison stand, prairie-strong and defiant.

December

For Creative Minds

Grassland Habitat

Prairies, seas of grass, or grasslands are huge areas of flat land covered with grass. Some grasslands have tall grass, some short, and some have mixed grasses.

Fire is an important process in grassland habitats. As plant matter is burned off above ground, ash provides nutrients to the soil and nitrogen is released below ground. As a result, new plant shoots that emerge after the burn are more nutritious for wildlife and livestock. Fire also prevents trees and shrubs from taking over the grassland. Lightning can cause wildfires, especially if weather conditions are dry and windy.

Grasslands receive an average of 10 to 40 inches (about 25 to 100 cm) of precipitation each year. Less rain would turn the grassland to desert and more rain would allow more trees to grow into forests.

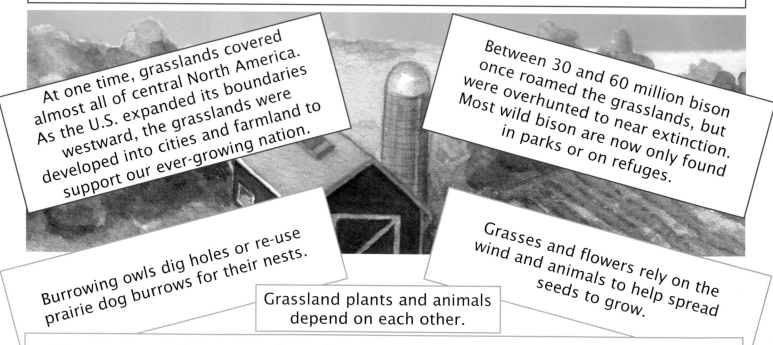

At one time, grasslands covered almost all of central North America. As the U.S. expanded its boundaries westward, the grasslands were developed into cities and farmland to support our ever-growing nation.

Between 30 and 60 million bison once roamed the grasslands, but were overhunted to near extinction. Most wild bison are now only found in parks or on refuges.

Burrowing owls dig holes or re-use prairie dog burrows for their nests.

Grassland plants and animals depend on each other.

Grasses and flowers rely on the wind and animals to help spread seeds to grow.

The grasses get their energy from the sun, water, and the fertile soil. Prairie chickens, groundhogs, deer, and bison all eat the grass. Eagles, foxes, cougars, and coyotes eat some of the plant-eating animals. When they die, their bodies decay and the nutrients return to the soil to help the plants grow.

For more detailed food web information and activities, go to the book's free online activities.

Grasslands Around the World

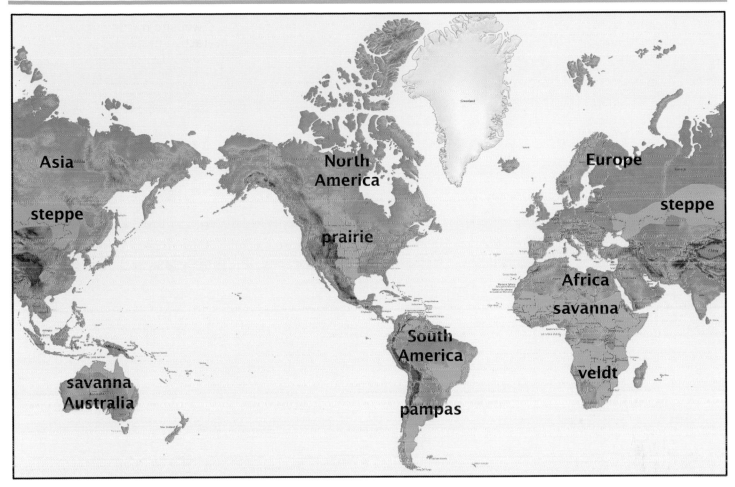

We call them prairies in North America, but grasslands are known by different names in other parts of the world. Using the map, see if you can answer these questions. Answers are upside down, below.

1 What are grasslands in South America called?

2 Savannas and veldts are names for grasslands on what continent?

3 On what continents are steppes?

4 What are grasslands called in Australia?

Answers: 1) pampas, 2) Africa, 3) Europe and Asia, 4) savanna

Weather or Season?

Weather changes quickly. Sometimes it can be sunny and hot in the morning but thunderstorms might pop up in the afternoon. Weather is usually reported on an hourly (internet) or daily basis.

Seasons affect weather too. Not only does the temperature change from one season to another, but the type or frequency of precipitation changes too.

Match the description to the appropriate weather or season. Answers are upside down at the bottom of the page.

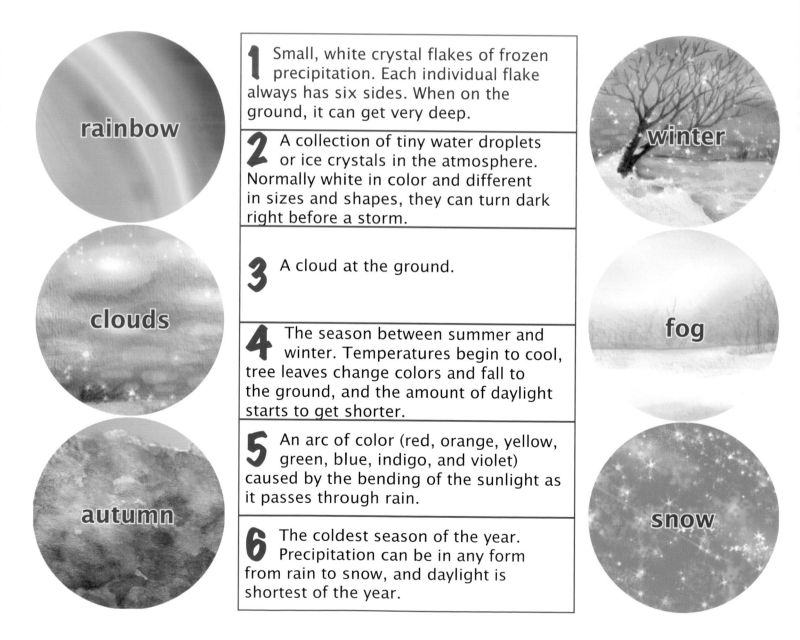

rainbow

clouds

autumn

winter

fog

snow

1 Small, white crystal flakes of frozen precipitation. Each individual flake always has six sides. When on the ground, it can get very deep.

2 A collection of tiny water droplets or ice crystals in the atmosphere. Normally white in color and different in sizes and shapes, they can turn dark right before a storm.

3 A cloud at the ground.

4 The season between summer and winter. Temperatures begin to cool, tree leaves change colors and fall to the ground, and the amount of daylight starts to get shorter.

5 An arc of color (red, orange, yellow, green, blue, indigo, and violet) caused by the bending of the sunlight as it passes through rain.

6 The coldest season of the year. Precipitation can be in any form from rain to snow, and daylight is shortest of the year.

Answers: 1) snow, 2) clouds, 3) fog, 4) autumn (fall), 5) rainbow, 6) winter

precipitation

7	A fast spinning column of air that reaches from a cloud to the ground, usually during a thunderstorm. These very dangerous storms are sometimes called twisters.
8	Small drops of liquid precipitation.
9	Water that falls from clouds. Depending on the season and temperature, it can fall as rain, sleet, hail, or snow.
10	A type of storm with thunder and lightning. There may or may not be rain, hail, or wind.
11	An electrical explosion made by a thunderstorm. The explosion's sound is called thunder.
12	The season between winter and summer. Temperature begins to warm, tree leaves grow green, flowers start to bloom, daylight gets longer.
13	The hottest season of the year. Afternoon thunderstorms can pop up, there's more daylight than darkness each day.
14	Frozen ice balls of precipitation from thunderstorms. Most are small but some can be as big as softballs!

thunderstorm

hail

spring

lightning

tornado

rain

summer

Animals, Weather and Seasonal Changes: True or False?

Can you tell which statements are true and which are false? Answers are upside down, below.

1 Prairie chickens dig a roost in a snowdrift.

2 Groundhogs migrate to warmer climates in the winter and come back in the spring.

3 Sandhill cranes migrate.

4 Prairie dogs stay in their underground burrows, out of the rain.

5 Some animals run for cover from rain or hail. They may hide in their den or may huddle under trees or bushes.

6 Skunks stay in their burrows during the cold seasons. When it is hot, they only come out at night, when it is cooler.

7 Burrowing owls hibernate to avoid cold weather.

8 Some animals grow thicker fur to keep them warm in the winter.

Answers: 1) True, 2) False—groundhogs hibernate for the winter, 3) True, 4) True, 5) True, 6) True, 7) False—burrowing owls migrate, 8) True

Humans, Weather, and Seasonal Changes

Can you answer these questions? Answers are upside down, below.

1 A meteorologist studies and predicts the weather. True or False?

2 Which instrument is used to measure temperature: ruler, scale, or thermometer?

3 Humans wear warm clothes in the winter to stay warm. True or False?

4 Humans heat homes and buildings to stay warm in the summer. True or False?

5 What should you do if you hear thunder?

6 What should you do if you are under a tornado warning?

7 Which clouds might warn of rain: white fluffy clouds or dark clouds?

8 What weather event might start a fire on the prairie?

9 How can you stay dry when it rains?

10 What is a winter storm with wind speeds higher than 35 mph (56 km) and enough falling or blowing snow making it hard to see?

Answers: 1) True, 2) thermometer, 3) True, 4) False, humans heat buildings in the winter, not summer. 5) As soon as you hear thunder, you should get to safety—inside a house or car. If outside, stay away from single trees or metal objects and squat on the balls of your feet. Do not swim or take a bath. 6) If a tornado is near, you should go to a basement or an inside room/hall without windows. 7) dark clouds, 8) lightning, 9) use an umbrella or wear a raincoat, 10) blizzard

For Haileigh and Bruce—DP

For Vinnie, with gratitude—KR

Thanks to Dr. Jeff Masters, Director of Meteorology at Weather Underground, Inc. for checking the accuracy of the weather information; and to staff at the Tall Grass Prairie National Preserve for checking the accuracy of the prairie information.

Library of Congress Cataloging-in-Publication Data

Pattison, Darcy.
  Prairie storms / by Darcy Pattison ; illustrated by Kathleen Rietz.
      p. cm.
  ISBN 978-1-60718-129-3 (hardcover) -- ISBN 978-1-60718-139-2 (softcover) -- ISBN 978-1-60718-149-1 (english ebook) -- ISBN 978-1-60718-159-0 (spanish ebook) 1. Prairie ecology--United States--Juvenile literature. 2. Prairie animals--United States--Juvenile literature. 3. Storms--United States--Juvenile literature. I. Rietz, Kathleen, ill. II. Title.
  QH104.P38 2011
  577.4'40973--dc23
                          2011016339

Also available as eBooks featuring auto-flip, auto-read, 3D-page-curling, and selectable English and Spanish text and audio
Interest level: 004-009
Grade level: P-4
Lexile Level: 860 Lexile Code: AD
Curriculum keywords: adaptations, food web, habitat, human interaction: seasons, life science: general, seasons, time: month, weather, weather/climate, weather/seasons, weather: severe

Manufactured in China, June, 2011
This product conforms to CPSIA 2008
First Printing
Published by Sylvan Dell Publishing
Mt. Pleasant, SC 29464